the Alphabet Keeper

Keeper

Mary Murphy

Alfred A. Knopf ❦ New York

The Alphabet Keeper keeps all her letters caged in the dark.

One day she cleans the cage. The letters fly around the room, each letter making its own special sound.

There is a sudden gust of wind
and the window swings open. The letters feel
the delicious breeze. They shiver with excitement.

"Freedom at last!" they cry.

"Come back!" screams the Alphabet Keeper, but too late.

She grabs her hat and chases the flying letters.

The letters land in the park.
How lovely to feel the
air and the tickly grass!

The Alphabet Keeper sneaks up . . .

but **p** turns upside
down and the
park turns
into

bark.

Then **b** turns backward and the **bark** becomes **dark**.

"I can't see them!" says the Alphabet Keeper, and the letters fly away again.

"I'll chase them in the bus," says the Alphabet Keeper.

But **h** flies down . . .

and turns the **bus** into a **bush**.

"Okay then, a boat!"
she says, and jumps onto the deck.

But **u** swaps with **e** . . .

and the **deck** turns
into a **duck**.

The Alphabet
Keeper thinks.

"I have a plan," she says.
But **t** jumps down . . .

plan

and turns her
plan into a **plant**.

"Stupid plant!"
she yells, and kicks it.

Then **p** and **l** break away, and the **plant** turns into an **ant**.

"I'll hide behind this hedge," says the Alphabet Keeper.

f l i t z

h

But **h** flies away . . . .

jump

and the **hedge** turns into the **edge**, which the Alphabet Keeper falls over.

"Rats!"
she says, standing up.

But **rats**
flies around
and turns
into **star** . . .

and she falls down
again, dazzled.

"Where can we hide?" cry the letters.
"Shout loud!" says **c**.
"Loud!" shout the letters, and **c** jumps up and turns **loud** . . .

. . . into **cloud**.

The letters sit in the cloud, silent.

But the Alphabet Keeper nets
them, hiding in the cloud.

"You can all stay in here!" she says.
But **t** turns **here** into **there** . . .

and there they are, free again!

"I'll get you!"
shouts the Alphabet Keeper,
fixing her hat.

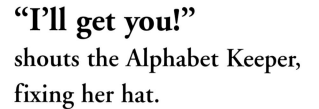

But **c** pushes

h away . . .

and turns her **hat**
into a **cat,** and the
Alphabet Keeper can't see.

Then **h** jumps back and
turns the **cat** into a **chat,**
and the Alphabet Keeper
has to wait
and talk.

my goodness!

awful weather indeed

well, well!

'STOP!'

shouts the
Alphabet Keeper.

But the letters jump
backward and
stop changes
into **pots,** which
fall on her.

CLANG

"You catch them, crow!"
says the Alphabet Keeper.

But **r** flies away, and **crow** turns into a **cow**.

"I've had enough!" screams the
Alphabet Keeper, throwing a rock at the letters.

"Quick!"
shout **e** and **t** . . .

and they turn the
rock into a **rocket**.

"**Moo!**" says the cow in shock, and down jumps **n** and turns **MOO** into . . .

. . . the **moon**.

And that's where
all the letters go
in the rocket.

And the Alphabet Keeper will never get them back.